An I Can Read
Picture Book™

Frog and Toad Together

by Arnold Lobel

SCHOLASTIC INC.

New York Toronto London Auckland Sydney
Mexico City New Delhi Hong Kong

For Barbara Dicks

ISBN 0-439-15833-8

Copyright© 1971, 1972 by Arnold Lobel. All rights reserved. Published by Scholastic Inc., 555 Broadway, New York, NY 10012, by arrangement with HarperCollins Publishers. SCHOLASTIC and associated logos are trademarks and/or registered trademarks of Scholastic Inc.

12 11 10 9 8 7 6 5 4 3 2 1   9/9 0 1 2 3 4/0

Printed in the U.S.A.   24

First Scholastic printing, October 1999

Typography by Tom Starace and David Horowitz.

Contents

A List

One morning Toad sat in bed. "I have many things to do," he said. "I will write them all down on a list so that I can remember them."

Toad wrote on a piece of paper:

A List of things to do today

Then he wrote:

Wake up

"I have done that," said Toad, and he crossed out:

~~Wake up~~

Then Toad wrote other things on the paper.

A List
of things to do
today

~~Wake up~~
Eat Breakfast
Get Dressed
Go to Frog's House
Take walk with Frog
Eat lunch
Take nap
Play games with Frog
Eat Supper
Go To Sleep

"There," said Toad. "Now my day is all written down."

He got out of bed and had something to eat. Then Toad crossed out:

~~Eat Breakfast~~

Toad took his clothes out of the closet and put them on.

Then he crossed out:

Toad put the list in his pocket.

He opened the door and walked out into
the morning. Soon Toad was at Frog's front
door. He took the list from his pocket and
crossed out:

~~Go to Frog's House~~

Toad knocked at the door.

"Hello," said Frog.

"Look at my list of things to do," said Toad.

"Oh," said Frog, "that is very nice."

Toad said, "My list tells me that we will go for a walk."

"All right," said Frog. "I am ready."

Frog and Toad went on a long walk. Then Toad took the list from his pocket again.

He crossed out:

~~Take walk with Frog~~

Just then there was a strong wind. It blew the list out of Toad's hand. The list blew high up into the air.

"Help!" cried Toad. "My list is blowing away. What will I do without my list?"

"Hurry!" said Frog. "We will run and catch it."

"No!" shouted Toad. "I cannot do that."

"Why not?" asked Frog.

"Because," wailed Toad, "running after my list is not one of the things that I wrote on my list of things to do!"

Frog ran after the list. He ran over hills and swamps, but the list blew on and on. At last Frog came back to Toad.

"I am sorry," gasped Frog, "but I could not catch your list."

"Blah," said Toad.

"I cannot remember any of the things that were on my list of things to do. I will just have to sit here and do nothing," said Toad.

Toad sat and did nothing. Frog sat with him.

After a long time Frog said, "Toad, it is getting dark. We should be going to sleep now."

"Go to sleep!" shouted Toad. "That was the last thing on my list!"

Toad wrote on the ground with a stick:

Go to sleep

Then he crossed out:

~~Go to sleep~~

"There," said Toad. "Now my day is all crossed out!"

"I am glad," said Frog.

Then Frog and Toad went right to sleep.

The Garden

Frog was in his garden. Toad came walking by. "What a fine garden you have, Frog," he said.

"Yes," said Frog. "It is very nice, but it was hard work."

"I wish I had a garden," said Toad.

"Here are some flower seeds. Plant them in the ground," said Frog, "and soon you will have a garden."

"How soon?" asked Toad.

"Quite soon," said Frog.

Toad ran home. He planted the flower seeds.

"Now seeds," said Toad, "start growing."

Toad walked up and down a few times. The
seeds did not start to grow.

Toad put his head close to the ground and said loudly, "Now seeds, start growing!"

Toad looked at the ground again. The seeds did not start to grow.

Toad put his head very close to the ground and shouted "NOW SEEDS, START GROWING!"

Frog came running up the path. "What is all this noise?" he asked.

"My seeds will not grow," said Toad.

"You are shouting too much," said Frog. "These poor seeds are afraid to grow."

"My seeds are afraid to grow?" asked Toad.

"Of course," said Frog. "Leave them alone for a few days. Let the sun shine on them, let the rain fall on them. Soon your seeds will start to grow."

That night Toad looked out of his window. "Drat!" said Toad. "My seeds have not started to grow. They must be afraid of the dark."

Toad went out to his garden with some candles. "I will read the seeds a story," said Toad. "Then they will not be afraid."

Toad read a long story to his seeds.

All the next day Toad sang
songs to his seeds.

And all the next day Toad read
poems to his seeds.

And all the next day Toad
played music for his seeds.

Toad looked at the ground. The seeds still did not start to grow.

"What shall I do?" cried Toad. "These must be the most frightened seeds in the whole world!"

Then Toad felt very tired, and he fell asleep.

"Toad, Toad, wake up," said Frog. "Look at your garden!"

Toad looked at his garden. Little green plants were coming up out of the ground.

"At last," shouted Toad, "my seeds have stopped being afraid to grow!"

"And now you will have a nice garden too," said Frog.

"Yes," said Toad, "but you were right, Frog. It was very hard work."

Cookies

Toad baked some cookies. "These cookies smell very good," said Toad. He ate one. "And they taste even better," he said.

Toad ran to Frog's house. "Frog, Frog," cried Toad, "taste these cookies that I have made."

Frog ate one of the cookies. "These are the best cookies I have ever eaten!" said Frog.

Frog and Toad ate many cookies, one after another.

"You know, Toad," said Frog, with his mouth full, "I think we should stop eating. We will soon be sick."

"You are right," said Toad. "Let us eat one last cookie, and then we will stop."

Frog and Toad ate one last cookie. There were many cookies left in the bowl.

"Frog," said Toad, "let us eat one very last cookie, and then we will stop."

Frog and Toad ate one very last cookie.

"We must stop eating!" cried Toad as he ate another.

"Yes," said Frog, reaching for a cookie, "we need will power."

"What is will power?" asked Toad.

"Will power is trying hard *not* to do
something that you really want to do,"
said Frog.

"You mean like trying *not* to eat all of these
cookies?" asked Toad.

"Right," said Frog.

Frog put the cookies in a box. "There," he said. "Now we will not eat any more cookies."

"But we can open the box," said Toad.

"That is true," said Frog.

Frog tied some string around the box. "There," he said. "Now we will not eat any more cookies."

"But we can cut the string and open the box," said Toad.

"That is true," said Frog.

Frog got a ladder. He put the box up on a high shelf. "There," said Frog. "Now we will not eat any more cookies."

"But we can climb the ladder and take the box down from the shelf and cut the string and open the box," said Toad.

"That is true," said Frog. Frog climbed the ladder and took the box down from the shelf. He cut the string and opened the box.

Frog took the box outside. He shouted in a loud voice, "HEY BIRDS, HERE ARE COOKIES!"

Birds came from everywhere. They picked up all the cookies in their beaks and flew away.

"Now we have no more cookies to eat," said Toad sadly. "Not even one."

"Yes," said Frog, "but we have lots and lots of will power."

"You may keep it all, Frog," said Toad. "I am going home now to bake a cake."

Dragons and Giants

Frog and Toad were reading a book together.

"The people in this book are brave," said Toad. "They fight dragons and giants, and they are never afraid."

"I wonder if we are brave," said Frog.

Frog and Toad looked into a mirror.

"We look brave," said Frog.

"Yes, but are we?" asked Toad.

Frog and Toad went outside.

"We can try to climb this mountain," said Frog. "That should tell us if we are brave."

Frog went leaping over rocks, and Toad came puffing up behind him.

They came to a dark cave. A big snake came out of the cave.

"Hello lunch," said the snake when he saw Frog and Toad. He opened his wide mouth. Frog and Toad jumped away. Toad was shaking.

"I am not afraid!" he cried.

They climbed higher, and they heard a loud noise. Many large stones were rolling down the mountain.

"It's an avalanche!" cried Toad.

Frog and Toad jumped away. Frog was trembling.

"I am not afraid!" he shouted.

They came to the top of the mountain. The
shadow of a hawk fell over them. Frog and Toad
jumped under a rock. The hawk flew away.

"We are not afraid!" screamed Frog and Toad at the same time. Then they ran down the mountain very fast.

They ran past the place where they saw the avalanche. They ran past the place where they saw the snake. They ran all the way to Toad's house.

"Frog, I am glad to have a brave friend like you," said Toad. He jumped into the bed and pulled the covers over his head.

"And I am happy to know a brave person like you, Toad," said Frog. He jumped into the closet and shut the door.

Toad stayed in the bed, and Frog stayed in the closet. They stayed there for a long time, just feeling very brave together.

The Dream

Toad was asleep, and he was having a dream. He was on a stage, and he was wearing a costume.

Toad looked out into the dark. Frog was sitting in the theater.

A strange voice from far away said, "PRESENTING THE GREATEST TOAD IN ALL THE WORLD!"

Toad took a deep bow.

Frog looked smaller as he shouted, "Hooray for Toad!"

"TOAD WILL NOW PLAY THE PIANO VERY WELL," said the strange voice.

Toad played the piano, and he did not miss a note. "Frog," cried Toad, "can you play the piano like this?"

"No," said Frog.

It seemed to Toad that Frog looked even smaller.

"TOAD WILL NOW WALK ON A HIGH WIRE,

AND HE WILL NOT FALL DOWN," said the voice.

Toad walked on the high wire. "Frog," cried
Toad, "can you do tricks like this?"

"No," peeped Frog, who looked very,
very small.

"TOAD WILL NOW DANCE, AND HE WILL BE

WONDERFUL," said the voice.

"Frog, can you be as wonderful as this?" said Toad as he danced all over the stage.

There was no answer.

Toad looked out into the theater. Frog was so small that he could not be seen or heard.

"Frog," said Toad, "where are you?"

There was still no answer.

"Frog, what have I done?" cried Toad.

Then the voice said, "THE GREATEST TOAD
WILL NOW . . ."

"Shut up!" screamed Toad. "Frog, Frog,
where have you gone?"

Toad was spinning in the dark.

"Come back, Frog," he shouted. "I will be
lonely!"

"I am right here," said Frog. Frog was standing near Toad's bed. "Wake up, Toad," he said.

"Frog, is that really you?" said Toad.

"Of course it is me," said Frog.

"And are you your own right size?" asked Toad.

"Yes, I think so," said Frog.

Toad looked at the sunshine coming through the window. "Frog," he said, "I am so glad that you came over."

"I always do," said Frog.

Then Frog and Toad ate a big breakfast. And
after that they spent a fine, long day together.